SKYLARK CHOOSE YOUR OWN ADVENTURE® · 20

"I DON'T LIKE CHOOSE YOUR OWN ADVENTURE® BOOKS. I *LOVE* THEM!" says Jessica Gordon, age 10. And now kids between the ages of six and nine can choose their own adventures too. Here's what kids have to say about the Skylark Choose Your Own Adventure® books.

"These are my favorite books because you can pick whatever choice you want—and the story is all about you."

—**Katy Alson,** *age 8*

"I love finding out how my story will end."

—**Joss Williams,** *age 9*

"I like all the illustrations!"

—**Savitri Brightfield,** *age 7*

"A six-year-old friend and I have lots of fun making the decisions together."

—**Peggy Marcus** *(adult)*

Bantam Skylark Books in the Choose Your Own
   Adventure® Series
Ask your bookseller for the books you have missed

TROUBLE IN SPACE

JOHN WOODCOCK

ILLUSTRATED BY RANDY JONES

An R.A. Montgomery Book

A BANTAM SKYLARK BOOK®
TORONTO · NEW YORK · LONDON · SYDNEY · AUCKLAND

RL 3, 007–009

TROUBLE IN SPACE
A Bantam Skylark Book/September 1984

CHOOSE YOUR OWN ADVENTURE® is a registered
trademark of Bantam Books, Inc.

Skylark Books is a registered trademark of
Bantam Books, Inc.
Registered in U.S. Patent and Trademark Office
and elsewhere.

Original conception of Edward Packard

ISBN 0-553-15271-8

Published simultaneously in the United States and Canada

Bantam Books are published by Bantam Books, Inc. Its trademark, consisting of the words "Bantam Books" and the por-
trayal of a rooster, is Registered in U.S. Patent and Trademark
Office and in other countries. Marca Registrada. Bantam
Books, Inc., 666 Fifth Avenue, New York, New York 10103.

PRINTED IN THE UNITED STATES OF AMERICA

CW   0 9 8 7 6 5 4 3 2

*For Erica,
Alison, and Steve*

READ THIS FIRST!!!

Most books are about other people.

This book is about you—and your space adventures.

Do not read this book from the first page through to the last page.

Instead, start at page one and read until you come to your first choice. Decide what you want to do. Then turn to the page shown and see what happens.

When you come to the end of a story, go back and try another choice. Every choice leads to a new adventure.

Have fun in space—and good luck!

You live with your parents in a small space station high above Earth. Your parents are members of the Galaxy Rescue Squad. The Squad helps anyone—or anything—in trouble in space. Right now, your parents are on a rescue mission near the edge of the galaxy.

But you're not alone. Staying with you is your friend Xmax. Xmax is a Zoonick from a faraway planet called Zoon. He looks like a large, furry egg, and he has a brain like a computer.

Xmax is helping you with your math homework when an emergency call comes in. It's from Galaxy Rescue Squad headquarters.

"A spaceship is in trouble," they tell you. "It's lost its power. It's drifting away from the solar system!"

Your parents can't answer this emergency call. But maybe you can!

Turn to page 2.

2 "YOUR PARENTS WANT YOU TO BE HERE WHEN THEY RETURN," Xmax warns.

"They could be gone for weeks!" you say. "We have plenty of time to answer the call."

Then there's another message from Squad headquarters: "Drifting ship may be from Zoon." That settles it—Xmax agrees to go.

You and the Zoonick climb into the extra space pod. You switch on the power—and you're ready to blast off! But what course should you take?

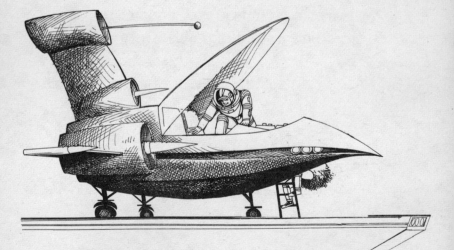

Go on to the next page.

"THE FASTER ROUTE HAS NOT BEEN **3** FULLY EXPLORED," Xmax says. "THE SLOWER ROUTE WOULD BE SAFER."

But if you take the slower way, your parents may get back to the space station before you do—which means trouble.

If you take the faster way, though, you might not get back at all. . . .

If you decide to take the slower, safer way, turn to page 20.

If you decide to take the faster way, turn to page 8.

4 "WHILE WE WERE SLEEPING," Xmax says, "THE AUTOMATIC PILOT DROVE US OUT OF OUR GALAXY."

"We'll turn the space pod around," you say, "and hibernate until we get back to the space station."

"WE CAN'T," says Xmax. "WE'VE USED UP ALL THE HIBERNATION GAS. THAT'S WHY WE WOKE UP."

"How far from Earth are we?" you ask.

"WE HAVE BEEN TRAVELING THROUGH SPACE FOR FIFTY YEARS," Xmax answers.

Go on to the next page.

And it will take fifty years to get back! If you **5** don't hibernate, you'll be fifty years older when you get there. . . .

Is there any point to going back? Maybe you should go on. At least you'll have a great adventure. Or should you return? Whether you're older or not, Earth *is* your home.

If you decide to travel on, turn to page 40.

If you decide to start back to Earth, turn to page 25.

There's no way to tell where the ice is thick **7**
enough for the space pod to land. You'll land
on the wing of the spaceship instead.

The pod touches down. You and Xmax step
out onto the wing. A door opens slowly in the
side of the ship. The two of you walk through it.
Suddenly the door slams closed behind you!
"More Galaxy Rescue Squad members," a
voice booms at you. "We have quite a collec-
tion of them."

"SPACE PIRATES!" Xmax mutters.

"Clever Zoonick," says the voice.

Now a door slides open in front of you. Four
more Squad members are standing there . . .
and two of them are your parents!

Turn to page 30.

8   You're afraid that the drifting spaceship will be lost if you don't hurry. "We'll take the faster route," you tell Xmax.

The space pod's controls are set for full speed. You blast away from the space station. Then you turn on the automatic pilot and head in a straight line toward the drifting spaceship.

Since this part of space hasn't been mapped, you're not sure what to expect.

Hours pass with no problems.

"Everything seems okay," you tell Xmax. "We can just sit back and relax."

You've flown past Venus, and you're nearing Jupiter. Suddenly lots of tiny dots begin to flash on your radar screen!

Turn to page 24.

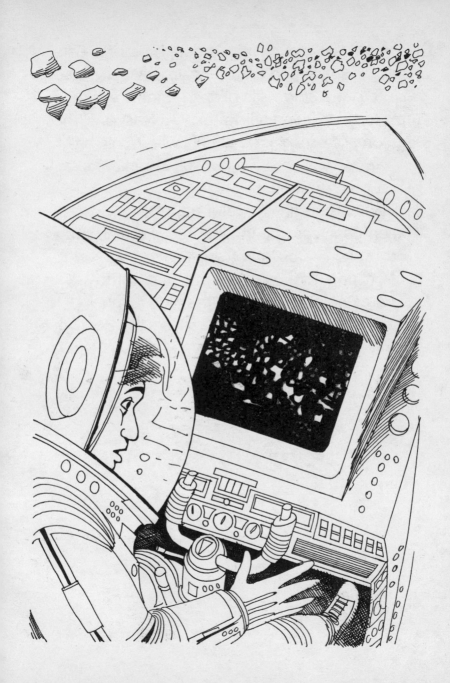

10   You really haven't had enough practice driving the space pod. You'd better leave the hard stuff to the automatic pilot. "I think we should try to sleep," you tell Xmax. "At least until the automatic pilot gets us out of this asteroid belt."

Xmax switches on some soft Zoonian music. You both doze off.

When you finally wake up, you can hardly keep your eyes open. The radar screen must be broken—you don't see any planets on it. Then you look outside the pod at the sky. There's nothing out there that you recognize!

"Xmax, wake up!" You shake the Zoonick awake. "Something's happened. I don't know where we are!"

Xmax rubs his eyes for a minute. Then he says: "ALL THAT BUMPING IN THE ASTEROID BELT. IT MUST HAVE RELEASED THE HIBERNATION GAS. WE'VE BEEN HIBERNATING!"

Turn to page 4.

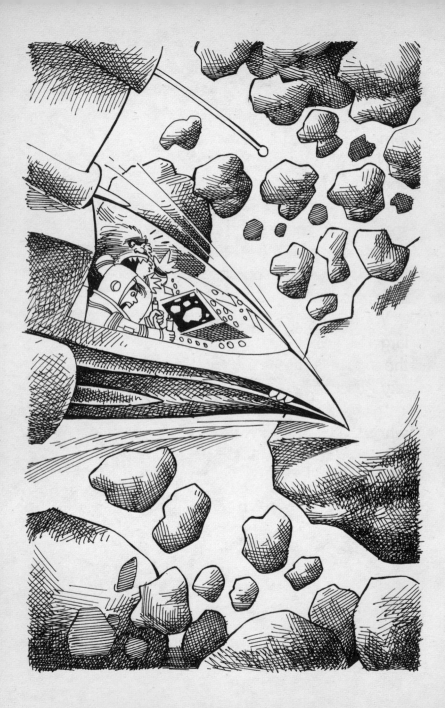

You really can't stand another minute of this **13** roller coaster ride. "I can do better than this machine!" you tell Xmax. You click off the automatic pilot and grab the controls.

Now it's like playing a video game that's going too fast—you don't even have time to think before an asteroid is right in front of the space pod. You steer the pod down. There's another asteroid! You jerk the wheel to the left . . . another! It's too late! You're going to hit it . . . SLAM!

Your space pod has crashed into one of the larger asteroids. The engines are wrecked. And the radio is a mess. You can't even call the Galaxy Rescue Squad for help!

"Stuck on an asteroid in the middle of nowhere!" you say to Xmax. "*Now* what are we supposed to do?"

Turn to page 22.

14   Jupiter has sixteen moons. Callisto is one of the larger ones. It's also shiny—although the inside of Callisto is red-hot, the outside is covered with rock and ice.

As your space pod flies closer, you see a dark-blue spaceship next to a mountain of ice. "What could be wrong with it?" you wonder. "It doesn't look as if it's crashed or anything."

"I DON'T HAVE A GOOD FEELING . . ." Xmax says.

But you aren't paying attention. Where should you land? You could set the pod down on the big, flat wing of the spaceship. But what if it *is* a pirate ship? They could capture you easily.

Maybe you should check things out first. But the bottom of your space pod is very hot. If you land, you might melt the ice on Callisto. Then the space pod might sink!

---

*If you decide to land on the ship's wing,
turn to page 7.*

*If you decide to land on the ice,
turn to page 26.*

"I think we'll take our chances with the as- **15** teroids," you tell Xmax.

"CORRECT CHOICE," Xmax agrees. "JUPITER IS A BAD PLACE."

But soon you're not sure you *have* made the right choice. As you squeeze in and out between asteroids, the space pod is bouncing around like a tennis ball. You're starting to feel very queasy. Even Xmax is looking a little green.

Maybe if you turn off the automatic pilot and take the controls yourself, you can smooth out the ride. Of course, you haven't had that much practice. What if you hit an asteroid? On the other hand, if this bouncing keeps up much longer, you're going to be really spacesick— and what good is a sick rescue squad?

Go on to the next page.

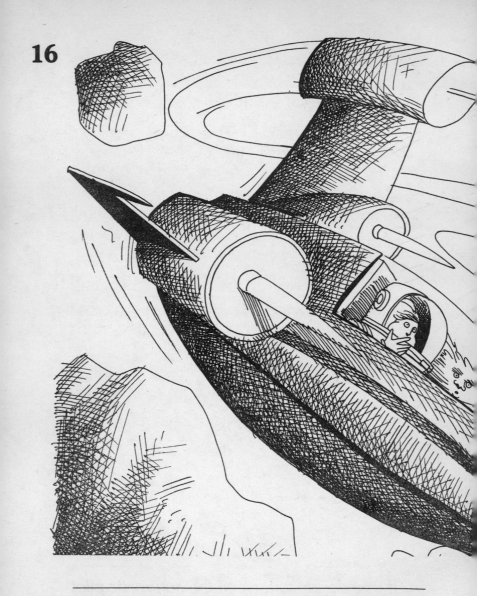

If you decide that you'd better stick with the automatic pilot, turn to page 10.

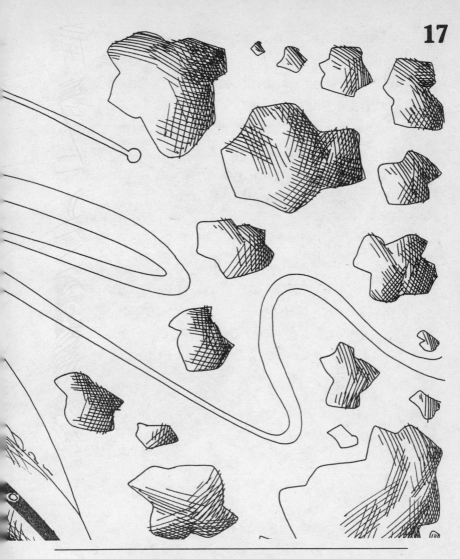

*If you decide to turn off the automatic pilot
and take over the pod's controls
yourself, turn to page 13.*

18   The Zoonicks need more power to pull away from the black hole. In the space pod you have the emergency equipment they need. But how will you get it to them?

You can see the Zoonian spaceship now—it's egg-shaped, like the Zoonicks themselves. And it's circling around an area even darker than space—a black hole!

You could take the emergency equipment to the ship in the rescue pod. But you might get sucked into the black hole yourself.

What if you use small rockets to launch the stuff to the Zoonicks? If that doesn't work, though, and the emergency equipment is lost, the Zoonick ship will end up in the black hole for sure.

If you decide to fly the space pod to the drifting spaceship, turn to page 45.

If you launch the emergency equipment to the ship, turn to page 35.

Driving the space pod through the asteroid **19** belt would be asking for trouble. "Let's take our chances with Jupiter," you say to Xmax.

"JUPITER IS DANGEROUS," Xmax warns. But you've already turned the space pod away from the asteroids. You'll be careful not to fly too close to the huge planet.

Suddenly your radio picks up an emergency signal. Xmax decodes the message.

"A CALL FOR HELP," he says. "ANOTHER SHIP IS DOWN ON CALLISTO." Callisto is one of Jupiter's moons.

"Let's find it!" you say.

"IT COULD BE A TRICK," Xmax warns. "THERE ARE SPACE PIRATES IN THIS PART OF THE SOLAR SYSTEM."

But you have to at least take a look. You lock the automatic pilot onto the emergency signal. It will steer your space pod right to the ship on Callisto.

Turn to page 14.

20   "Anything might happen if we take the fast route to the spaceship," you tell Xmax. "But if we go the slower way, I'm pretty sure we'll get there in one piece."

And you do! The trip takes days, but it's safe. You're just coming up on the planet Pluto when you hear an emergency signal. It's loud and clear. That means that the missing spaceship hasn't drifted too far out of the solar system. You'll be able to find it.

And the ship *is* Zoonian. Xmax picks up a radio message.

Go on to the next page.

"The ship is going in circles!" cries the captain. "It's being pulled closer and closer to a black hole. If the ship is dragged into the hole, it will be crushed. Or it will be sucked out of this galaxy, into another time and space—lost forever!"

You are the Zoonicks' only hope!

Turn to page 18.

22 "WE HAVE THREE CHOICES," Xmax says. "WE CAN USE SOME OF THE EQUIPMENT WE WERE CARRYING TO THE DRIFTING SHIP TO REPAIR OUR OWN ENGINES. BUT," he adds, "THAT EQUIPMENT IS FOR A MUCH LARGER SPACESHIP. IT COULD BE *TOO* POWERFUL. . . ."

"The second choice?" you ask.

"WE CAN BLOW UP THE SPACE POD," Xmax says, "AFTER WE USE OUR ROCKET VESTS TO JET TO ANOTHER ASTEROID. SPACE TRAVELERS WOULD PROBABLY NOTICE A BIG EXPLOSION AND COME TO TAKE A LOOK."

"Choice three?" you ask.

"WE CAN SIT HERE," Xmax says. "CHANCES ARE ONE IN A TRILLION THAT SOMEONE WILL PASS BY IN YOUR LIFETIME."

Go on to the next page.

Great. So should you use the equipment to **23** try to repair your engines? If it's too powerful, the space pod—and you and Xmax—could be in big trouble.

Or should you blow up the wrecked space pod and hope that will bring help?

If you decide to try to repair the engines, turn to page 36.

If you decide to blow up the space pod, turn to page 32.

24   The radar screen shows an asteroid belt dead ahead. Asteroids are enormous rocks, thousands of them, tumbling through space. Some of them are big enough to crush the space pod.

But if you turn the ship toward Jupiter to get away from the asteroids, you could be in worse trouble. There are terrible storms around the giant planet.

If you decide to take your chances with the asteroids, turn to page 15.

If you decide to go around the asteroid belt, turn to page 19.

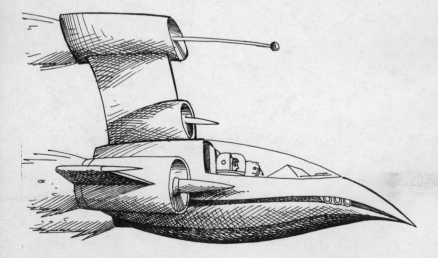

"Let's turn back," you say to Xmax. "I don't care how old I'll be when we get there. It's still my home!"

Fifty years pass—sometimes quickly, sometimes very slowly. You change a lot as the years go by. But Xmax doesn't change at all. Zoonicks never get older.

You see a few spaceships. But mostly it's you and Xmax alone in space. He teaches you lots of other space languages. And you get almost as good at math as a Zoonick.

But often you're lonely. You begin to wonder if you made the right choice after all.

Turn to page 47.

"I think we should land the space pod away from the ship," you tell Xmax. "In case there's anything funny about it."

"I DON'T LIKE EITHER CHOICE," Xmax grumbles.

You fly past the ice mountain and set the

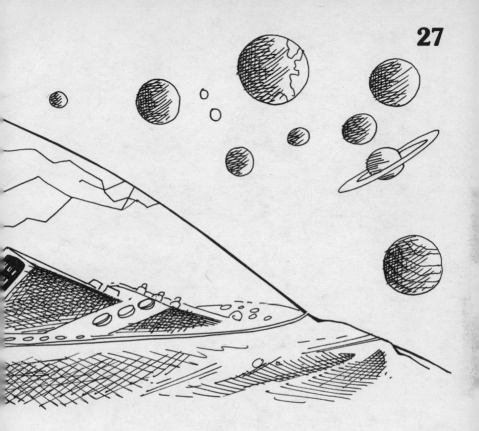

pod down. "It looks solid enough here," you say. Xmax doesn't say anything. The two of you climb out of the pod. "We'll sneak up on the ship—see what's going on," you say.

Turn to page 29.

But you haven't gone far when you hear a **29** strange noise: SLU-U-URPPP. It's the pod. It's sinking into the ice!

"They'd *better* be space pirates," you say to Xmax. "Because if something really is wrong with that ship, we could all be spending a lot of time on Callisto!"

The End

30 "Mom! Dad! What are *you* doing here?" you shout.

"We could ask you the same thing!" your father says.

"Xmax and I were going to rescue a drifting Zoonian spaceship. Then we heard an emergency signal on Callisto," you tell him. "We came down to see if we could help." You add, "I *did* finish all my homework before we left the station."

"WHAT DO THE SPACE PIRATES WANT?" Xmax asks.

"Our space pods, for spare parts," your mother says. "They'll let us out at the space station near Neptune." And the spaceship soon blasts off.

You were tricked by the pirates. But your parents were, too. So you don't feel too bad. And you weren't really in any danger . . . except maybe *now*, from your mom and dad. They're a little upset with you.

You have a feeling that this was your first and last rescue mission.

The End

"The emergency equipment would probably melt these little engines," you say. "The space suits will keep us going for a week. Let's blow up the space pod—I'm sure that will bring the Galaxy Rescue Squad straight to us."

You'd better be right.

Xmax turns the space pod into a big bomb. Then both of you climb out of the pod and strap on your rocket vests. You jet into space and head for another asteroid. Once you're there, you huddle in a crater and wait for the big bang.

Turn to page 34.

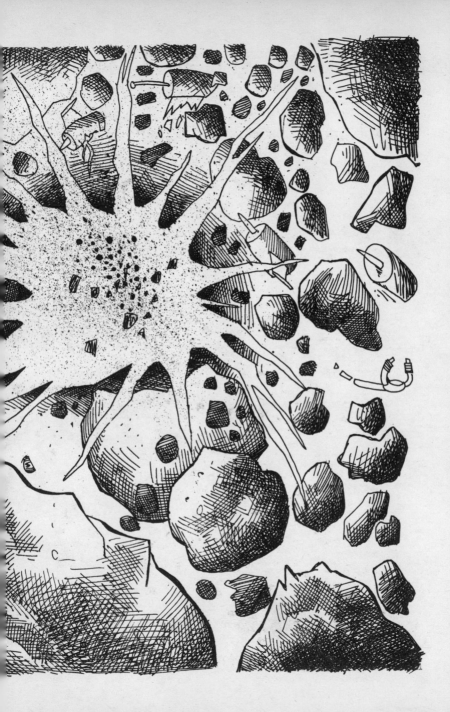

34   BLAM ! KA-POW! The pod explodes. So does the asteroid it crashed into. There's a giant cloud of smoke and dust. But if someone doesn't notice it soon, you'll never be found.

Turn to page 38.

Flying the equipment to the drifting ship **35** would be too dangerous. Your space pod would probably be sucked right into the black hole. And that would be the end of things for you *and* the Zoonicks.

"We'd better not get any closer," you say. "We'll launch the stuff to them." You and Xmax load the emergency equipment into three small rockets. Then you take aim and fire them out of the pod, one at a time.

Turn to page 48.

36   "We'll repair the space pod," you decide. All you want to do is get back to the space station.

You help Xmax put the wrecked engines together, using parts from the emergency equipment. Then, "TURN ON THE POWER," Xmax says. The engines hum. "EASE AWAY FROM THE ASTEROID," says the Zoonick, "VERY SLOWLY."

It works! Somehow you make your way back out of the asteroid belt.

"Home!" you say with a smile. You push the power drive all the way down.

Go on to the next page.

"NO!" Xmax shouts. But it's too late. You're **37** going faster . . . faster . . . so fast that everything in the sky is a blur. You can't turn off the engines!

There's a terrible roaring noise. "Now what?!" you shout.

The space pod feels as though it's shaking apart. "JUST HOPE THAT THE ENGINES WEAR OUT BEFORE THE POD DOES," Xmax says.

You promise yourself you'll be more careful next time, if there *is* a next time. . . .

The End

You're lucky! The cloud from the explosion shows up on the huge radar screen at Galaxy Rescue Squad headquarters. You and Xmax are only on the asteroid for a few hours when you see a space pod heading in your direction.

You and Xmax turn on your rocket vests,

and the Rescue Squad picks you up in the sky.
They tell you another space pod is on its way to
help the drifting spaceship.

Turn to page 43.

40   "Xmax," you say, "I think we should go on. Who knows? Perhaps there are beings in the next galaxy with superfast ships—fast enough to get us back to Earth before I'm too old." (Zoonicks like Xmax don't get any older.)

In the meantime, you'll both have lots to see. You set the automatic pilot toward a flat green galaxy in the distance.

Maybe someday kids will read about the two of you in their history books: you and Xmax, the first space explorers to travel to another galaxy and return to tell the tale.

The End

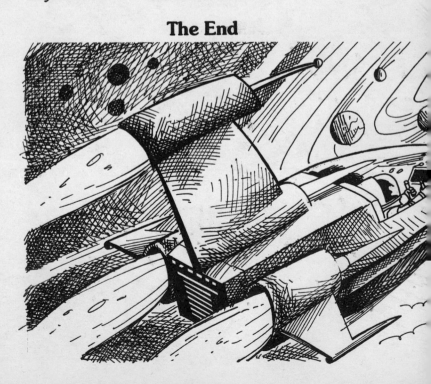

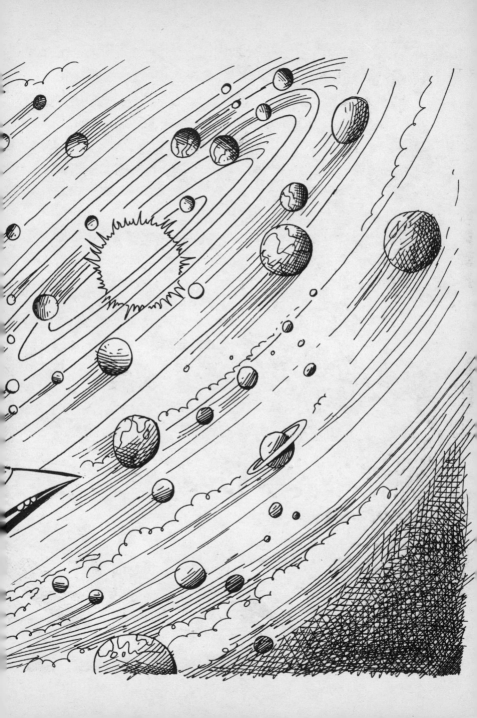

You're feeling pretty good until you re- **43** member: You wrecked a space pod on an asteroid. Then you blew it up! "About how much does one of these pods cost?" you ask the pilot.

"Sixty million dollars or so," she says. You gulp.

"HOW LONG DO YOU THINK IT WILL TAKE YOU TO PAY FOR IT OUT OF YOUR ALLOWANCE?" Xmax whispers. "IT'S A LITTLE MATH PROBLEM FOR YOU." He gives a quiet Zoonick chuckle.

The End

You decide there isn't time to play it safe.
"We're going in!" you tell Xmax.

You fly the space pod right over to the Zoonian spaceship. You dock with it and drop the emergency equipment down to the waiting Zoonicks.

Quickly they hook it up to their engines. Now the pod and the spaceship are both ready to blast away from the black hole.

Full power . . . the black hole is tugging at you . . . you feel as though the pod is made of solid lead. Slowly, slowly, you pull away. The spaceship does, too. Your first rescue mission, and it worked!

"I think this rescue business is pretty easy!" you shout to Xmax.

"THEN THINK AGAIN," Xmax says sternly. "THINK WHAT WOULD HAVE HAPPENED IF IT *HADN'T* WORKED."

In your mind, you see a tiny space pod tumbling into the blackness of the black hole . . . and you're inside it, looking out.

The End

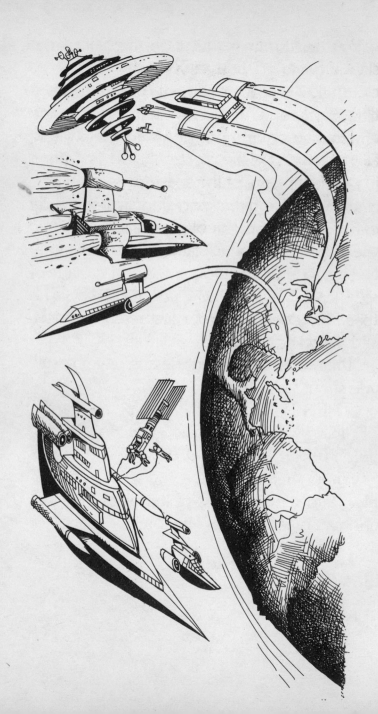

You and Xmax get to see all the things you slept through on your trip out: strange-colored clouds millions of miles across; planets with three suns and forty moons; stars that blink on and off like warning lights. But the best thing of all is at the end of the trip: Earth, growing larger in the sky in front of the space pod.

You're looking forward to getting there, of course. But you've been gone for a hundred years. Everything will be different now. You feel a little sad.

"IT WILL BE SAD, BUT ALSO INTEREST-ING," Xmax tells you. "WHEN WE LAND, WE WILL BE LOOKING AT THE FUTURE."

What will it be like? You're about to find out.

The End

48 There goes the first rocket: bull's-eye! Right into a round door on the side of the Zoonian spaceship. The second rocket fires. Another bull's-eye!

But when you fire the third rocket, something goes wrong. "Oh, no!" you shout. The rocket is veering away from the spaceship. It does a nose dive straight into the black hole. . . .

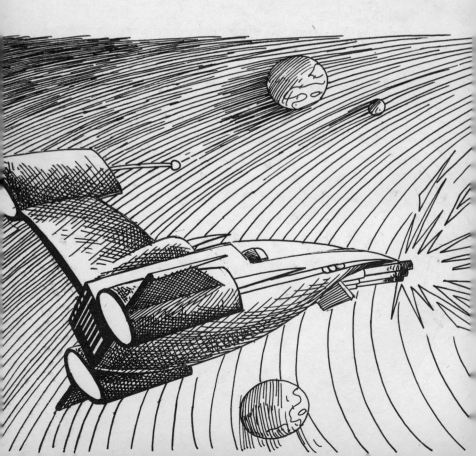

Now the Zoonian spaceship is being dragged closer to the black hole as well. But how can you help them? Even if you flew the pod to the ship, it wouldn't do any good—the equipment is lost!

"What should we do?" you ask Xmax.

"JUST WAIT," he says.

Go on to the next page.

50   Suddenly one of the spaceship's engines roars to life. The Zoonicks were able to repair one engine! Will they be able to pull away?

They do!

"Lucky for us that Zoonicks can fix almost anything!" you shout.

"LUCKY FOR *THEM*, YOU MEAN," says Xmax.

The End

ABOUT THE AUTHOR

John Woodcock grew up on Long Island, New York, but for the last thirteen years he has lived mostly in Bloomington, Indiana, where he teaches literature and writing at Indiana University. He also teaches courses about science and the future. He has worked as a writer for several environmental and arts organizations. Mr. Woodcock likes photography, singing, stargazing, sailing, reading, and cats. He and his wife have three children.

Now you can have your favorite Choose Your Own Adventure® Series in a variety of sizes. Along with the popular pocket size, Bantam has introduced the Choose Your Own Adventure® series in a Skylark edition and also in Hardcover.

Now not only do you get to decide on how you want your adventures to end, you also get to decide on what size you'd like to collect them in.

SKYLARK EDITIONS

☐ 15238	The Circus #1 E. Packard	$1.95
☐ 15207	The Haunted House #2 R. A. Montgomery	$1.95
☐ 15208	Sunken Treasure #3 E. Packard	$1.95
☐ 15233	Your Very Own Robot #4 R. A. Montgomery	$1.95
☐ 15308	Gorga, The Space Monster #5 E. Packard	$1.95
☐ 15309	The Green Slime #6 S. Saunders	$1.95
☐ 15195	Help! You're Shrinking #5 E. Packard	$1.95
☐ 15201	Indian Trail #8 R. A. Montgomery	$1.95
☐ 15191	The Genie In the Bottle #10 J. Razzi	$1.95
☐ 15222	The Big Foot Mystery #11 L. Sonberg	$1.95
☐ 15223	The Creature From Millers Pond #12 S. Saunders	$1.95
☐ 15226	Jungle Safari #13 E. Packard	$1.95
☐ 15227	The Search For Champ #14 S. Gilligan	$1.95
☐ 15241	Three Wishes #15 S. Gilligan	$1.95
☐ 15242	Dragons! #16 J. Razzi	$1.95
☐ 15261	Wild Horse Country #17 L. Sonberg	$1.95
☐ 15262	Summer Camp #18 J. Gitenstein	$1.95
☐ 15270	The Tower of London #19 S. Saunders	$1.95
☐ 15271	Trouble In Space #20 J. Woodcock	$1.95

Prices and availability subject to change without notice.

Buy them at your local bookstore or use this handy coupon for ordering:

DO YOU LOVE
CHOOSE YOUR OWN ADVENTURE®?

**Let your preschool-age brothers and sisters
in on the fun**

If you're a fan of CHOOSE YOUR OWN ADVENTURE
books and know preschoolers or beginning readers,
you can let them in on the fun by introducing them to
YOUR FIRST ADVENTURE™. YOUR FIRST ADVEN-
TURE books are similar to CHOOSE YOUR OWN
ADVENTURE, but they are designed for younger
boys and girls.

So now you can introduce your younger brothers
and sisters, or anyone else you know between the
ages of three and six, to the fun of reading CHOOSE
YOUR OWN ADVENTURE by telling them about
YOUR FIRST ADVENTURE.

YOUR FIRST ADVENTURE books are available
wherever Bantam paperbacks are sold.

SPECIAL
MONEY SAVING
OFFER

Now you can have an up-to-date listing of Bantam's hundreds of titles plus take advantage of our unique and exciting bonus book offer. A special offer which gives you the opportunity to purchase a Bantam book for only 50¢. Here's how!

By ordering any five books at the regular price per order, you can also choose any other single book listed (up to a $4.95 value) for just 50¢. Some restrictions do apply, but for further details why not send for Bantam's listing of titles today!

Just send us your name and address plus 50¢ to defray the postage and handling costs.

JIM KJELGAARD

In these adventure stories, Jim Kjelgaard shows us the special world of animals, the wilderness, and the bonds between men and dogs. *Irish Red* and *Outlaw Red* are stories about two champion Irish setters. *Snow Dog* shows what happens when a half-wild dog crosses paths with a trapper. The cougar-hunting *Lion Hound* and the greyhound story *Desert Dog* take place in our present-day Southwest. And, *Stormy* is an extraordinary story of a boy and his devoted dog. You'll want to read all these exciting books.